Rascal's Diet

For my wife, Lucy Curtin, who helped draft these stories
inspired by the animals of her own childhood.

First published in 2009
by Wayland

This paperback edition published in 2010 by Wayland

Text copyright © Peter Bently 2009
Illustration copyright © Elisabetta Ferrero 2009

Wayland
338 Euston Road
London NW1 3BH

Wayland Australia
Hachette Children's Books
Level 17/207 Kent Street
Sydney, NSW 2000

Series Editor: Louise John
Editor: Katie Powell
Cover design: Paul Cherrill
Design: D.R.ink
Consultant: Shirley Bickler

A CIP catalogue record for this book is available from the British Library.

ISBN 9780750256810 (hbk)
ISBN 9780750259927 (pbk)

Printed in China

Wayland is a division of Hachette Children's Books,
an Hachette UK Company

www.hachette.co.uk

Rascal's Diet

Written by Peter Bently
Illustrated by Elisabetta Ferrero

WAYLAND

One morning, Tara and Mum were in the big field. Plod and Rascal, the two horses, and Smokey the donkey, were having their breakfast.

Rocket, the sheepdog, was running around chasing butterflies.

Rascal finished her own breakfast, then stuck her nose into Smokey's bucket.

"Shoo, Rascal!" said Tara, pushing Rascal away. "Stop eating Smokey's food!"

"Rascal is too greedy," said Mum. "She's getting fat."

Later that morning, Tara took Rascal for a ride.

"Her saddle looks too tight!" said Mum.

"And she's too heavy to trot properly," said Tara.

"Right," said Mum. "The horse show is only a month away. Rascal needs to go on a diet!"

They put Rascal on her own in the small field.

"The grass is shorter here," said Mum. "There will be less for Rascal to eat."

"And she won't be able to steal Smokey's food!" said Tara.

So, Rascal lived on her own in the small field, while Plod and Smokey remained in the big field.

Rascal and her friends called to each other across the gate. Plod sometimes reached over to rub noses with Rascal.

One day, Tara was in the woods, climbing a tree.

From high up she could see all across Starcross Stables.

She saw Dad in the tractor, pulling a load of hay.

Mum was by the house, hanging out the washing. Rocket was chasing butterflies again.

Tara could also see the animals in their fields. Plod and Smokey were calling to Rascal over the gate.

Rascal was on the far side of her field. She neighed back to Plod and Smokey, but she didn't trot over to greet them.

"I wonder why Rascal isn't going to see her friends?" thought Tara.

She climbed down the tree and ran to the small field.

On the way she met Mum, who had finished hanging out the washing.

"Take Rascal's lunch with you," said Mum, handing Tara a bucket of food.

Tara opened the gate and
called, "Rascal!"
But Rascal didn't come.

She banged on the bucket, but Rascal still wouldn't respond.

"That's funny," thought Tara. "Rascal always comes for her food."

Tara carried the bucket to
Rascal on the far side of the
field. Instead of a hedge, there
was just a barbed-wire fence.

"Oh, Rascal, you poor thing!" said Tara, when she got close. "Your tail is caught in the fence. No wonder you can't move!"

Tara ran to fetch Mum, and together they set Rascal free.

Rascal trotted happily across the field to see Plod and Smokey.

"Look, she's trotting again," said Tara.

"Yes," said Mum. "Let's try her saddle on."

Tara fetched Rascal's saddle from the stables.
"It's not tight any more!" said Tara.

"No, it's just right," said Mum.
"The diet has worked well."

Tara rode Rascal back into the big field.

"Plod and Smokey will be delighted to have her back," said Tara.

"As long as she doesn't eat their dinner!" said Mum.

Tara and Rascal won lots of prizes at the horse show.

"It's lucky you can't eat rosettes, Rascal," said Tara.

"Yes," said Dad. "She's got so many she'd soon put on weight again!"

START READING is a series of highly enjoyable books for beginner readers. **The books have been carefully graded to match the Book Bands widely used in schools.** This enables readers to be sure they choose books that match their own reading ability.

Look out for the Band colour on the book in our Start Reading logo.

The Bands are:

Pink Band 1A & 1B

Red Band 2

Yellow Band 3

Blue Band 4

Green Band 5

Orange Band 6

Turquoise Band 7

Purple Band 8

Gold Band 9

START READING books can be read independently or shared with an adult. They promote the enjoyment of reading through satisfying stories supported by fun illustrations.

Peter Bently lives in Devon with his wife, Lucy and a ready-made audience of two children, Theo (9) and Tara (6). Apart from writing, he enjoys walking, going to the beach, meeting up with friends, and having family fun.

Elisabetta Ferrero works in Vercelli, a town in North Italy surrounded by paddy fields. She lives with her husband and two sons, a hunting dog who loves chasing rabbits but never catches them, six Burmese cats and a gold fish who is 11 years old!